S0-CPE-822

Ballet Magic

Nancy Robison
Illustrated by Karen Loccisano

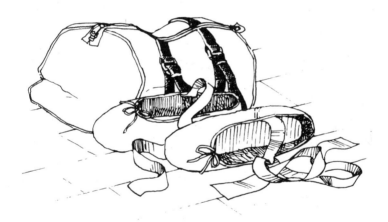

ALBERT WHITMAN & COMPANY
CHICAGO

Thanks to Shirley and Sharon,
my tall friends

Text © 1981 by Nancy Robison
Illustrations © 1981 by Karen Loccisano
Published simultaneously in Canada
by General Publishing, Limited, Toronto
All rights reserved. Printed in U.S.A.

Library of Congress Cataloging in Publication Data

Robison, Nancy.
  Ballet magic.

  (A Springboard book)
  Summary: Stacey's sudden spurt of growth makes
her feel unfit for ballet, until she learns that it
is possible to be both tall and graceful, and that
attitude is the most important element of dance.
  [1. Ballet—Fiction] I. Loccisano, Karen, ill.
II. Title   III. Series.
PZ7.R5697Bal   [Fic]   81-12921
ISBN 0-8075-0560-9   AACR2

Contents

I
Tallest Girl in Class

"Head up! Back straight!" Stacey's ballet teacher snapped.

Stacey sighed and straightened her spine. She tried not to slouch, but sometimes it was hard. She felt like a giraffe when she stood up straight.

In the past three months she'd grown almost three inches. She was a head taller than anyone else in her ballet class. She'd even passed up her brother, Tommy, who was a year older. He'd started to call her "Amazon Woman."

Stacey stood at the end of the *barre* and stretched her legs. She could look down the

4

lineup of girls and boys and see over their heads without standing on her toes.

"Second position, *plié*. Ready, begin." Ida May snapped her fingers to the count. "Up, down. Up, down."

Stacey squatted in the *plié* position and bent down in time with the count.

She had loved ballet ever since she was in the baby classes. A favorite exercise then was pretending to grow from a small tree into a big tree with spreading branches. How she wished she'd stayed the little tree instead of growing into a giant!

"*Rond de jambe en l'air,*" Ida May said. She always gave the ballet directions in French. The terms weren't hard to learn. *Rond de jambe* meant a circular movement of the leg. *En l'air* meant "in the air." It was fun to learn the French words. Stacey felt proud that she could remember them.

She stood on her right leg, holding the *barre* with her right hand, and swirled her left leg through the air.

"Straighten up!" Ida May shouted.

Stacey didn't need to ask who Ida May was talking to. She lifted her head and pulled up her rib cage. It was hard to stand tall when part of you really wanted to be invisible.

After a while Ida May waved one long graceful arm through the air. "Class to the center," she said. She wore her hair wound around her head in a braid and always held her chin high as she spoke. "Face the mirror."

This was the part of the lesson Stacey didn't like. She felt she stood out even more than when she was at the *barre*.

"*Assemblé*. Ready, begin!" Ida May said.

Stacey had done this basic step hundreds of times. She pushed off with two feet in a small jump, then brushed one foot in the air and joined both feet together in the landing. She cringed when she heard herself thump on the hardwood floor. After six years studying ballet, she should be getting better, not worse. But now that she was taller, there was more to lift up and more to bring down.

In front of her, Pam Hendricks and Lynn Woodson giggled. Were they laughing at her?

Stacey blushed.

Pam and Lynn were both small—the perfect size for dancers. They leaped around the ballet room like floating feathers. How could they ever understand what it felt like to be a giant?

Stacey had always been best friends with Pam. But in the past couple of years, Pam had been spending more time with Lynn. The two of them hardly ever paid attention to Stacey anymore. They'd gotten so close, they'd even started dressing alike. Today they were both wearing ice-blue leotards.

"Stop flapping your arms," Ida May said. "A ballet dancer moves her arms gracefully in a circular movement, not up and down like a bird about to fly."

Ida May wove in and out of the dancers, stopping to tip a head the right way or to straighten out someone's tense shoulders.

She clicked her fingers in time to the music. "Da-dum-de-dum-dum."

For fifteen minutes, the class bent down, straightened up, arched their backs, waved their arms, and traced circles on the floor with their toe shoes. Perspiration poured down Stacey's face. Would they ever stop?

Finally, Ida May said, "Take a break, class. I have an announcement to make."

Everyone sat down on the floor.

"As you know, the ballet recital this year will be *The Nutcracker*," she said.

Pam and Lynn nodded and smiled at each other.

Stacey smiled, too. For a few moments she could picture herself in a white tutu dancing the part of the Snow Queen. She'd always been a good dancer. How she loved swirling on her toes to the flow of the music!

But no, she thought, it was doubtful she'd be the Snow Queen. Lately, since she'd grown so much, her balance had been off. She'd been about as graceful as a snow goose.

"Who can tell us the story of *The Nutcracker?*" Ida May asked, looking around.

Pam raised her hand and Ida May asked her to go ahead.

"The story takes place at a Christmas party many years ago. A girl named Clara gets a toy from her godfather. I don't remember his name."

"Herr Drosselmeyer," Ida May said.

Pam continued, "The toy is a nutcracker, carved in the form of an old man. Clara's brother . . . I don't remember his name."

"Fritz," Ida May added.

"Yes, Fritz is jealous because Clara is given the toy to care for and he isn't. After the party, he throws the Nutcracker away. Clara dreams that she finds the toy and it has turned into a life-sized person—an old man with a wrinkled face."

"Would someone else like to tell what happens next?" Ida May asked.

Lynn popped to her feet. "I will," she said. "The Nutcracker takes Clara on a magical journey."

"Yes, go on," Ida May encouraged her.

"They go through the dark night to the land of Ice and Snow. But then, King Rat and some Mice attack and wound the Nutcracker. Clara chases the Mice away and goes back to help the poor old Nutcracker. Suddenly she sees he has turned into a young prince."

Ida May smiled. "Good. Now who would like to finish the tale?"

Stacey raised her hand. Ida May called on her.

"The Prince takes Clara to the magical Kingdom of Sweets, where she is presented to the Sugar Plum Fairy. Then there's a grand festival in Clara's honor. At the festival, the Sugar Plum Fairy, Gingerbread men, Candy Canes, Flowers, and others dance. After the party, Clara is returned home. She remembers this Christmas as the happiest of her life."

Ida May applauded. "Very good, class. You know the story well. The Nutcracker is a perfect ballet for us because it involves so many dancers. Jay Lanova's studio will be participating in the performance with us. Tryouts will begin in the middle of October—six weeks from now. We have a lot of work to do."

Stacey felt a sudden surge of panic. Just six more weeks till tryouts. That wasn't much time. How would she ever be ready? How could she ever prepare her clunky old body?

Ida May clapped her hands. "Okay, back to work, class!"

Everyone stood up and faced the mirror. Stacey stood behind Pam and Lynn. She overheard Pam say to Lynn in a loud whisper, "I wonder who will be the big old Nutcracker? I hope it isn't me!"

"Me too," Lynn answered. "But don't worry. We're too short. The Nutcracker has to be someone tall—like Stacey."

They looked at her but Stacey turned away fast. She didn't want them to know she had overheard them. She bent one knee and threw her hip out. It was one of the tricks she used to look shorter. But she could never fool Ida May.

"Stand up straight," Ida May yelled. "Dancers keep a straight back." She ran her fingers down Stacey's spine.

Stacey pulled her shoulders back until they ached. She felt she couldn't stand any straighter without breaking.

"Dancing is like magic," Ida May said to the class. "There's a trick to perfection and it's called hard work. A magician practices all the time to learn sleight of hand. Dancers must practice to make dancing look easy. They must work and work to look like clouds sweeping across the sky, not like a herd of cattle clopping across the stage. Now, let's dance!"

Ida May dropped the needle onto the record and the music began. "An-nd one . . . an-nd two . . ."

Stacey stepped up on *pointe.* As she did, she felt the familiar painful tingling sensation in her toes and a tightening in her calves. Would she ever get used to the pain of dancing on her toes?

The dance combination was one the class had done many times before, but after the first step, Stacey lost her balance and fell behind. She tried to catch up by watching the other students in the mirror but she only got confused and gave up. Out of the corner of her eye she saw Pam and Lynn giggle again.

They didn't help. She felt more self-conscious than ever.

Ida May scolded her in a loud whisper. "Why did you stop?"

Stacey was sure her face was red. She shrugged. "I just forgot what to do next!"

"Never quit!" Ida May turned to the rest of the class. "A dancer keeps going no matter what. Now let's try the combination again. Remember to point your toes and raise your free arm gracefully over your head. Face front. An-nd - da dum . . . ."

Stacey started doing the steps along with everyone else. She opened her feet into second position, stretched onto *pointe,* then did a running glide step followed by chain turns. She finished a beat behind everyone else.

Ida May noticed.

"Let's try the combination again, class," she said. She stood close to Stacey and spoke in her ear. "Now think about the position of your legs. Do the step with me." She took Stacey's hand and went through the steps with her. "That's it."

Slowing down the steps made it easier for Stacey to follow, though her feet seemed to hurt more when she danced so carefully. Maybe she'd been messing up because she was hurrying to get off her toes. That might be part of the problem, anyway.

After Ida May dismissed class, Stacey sat down to take off her shoes. It felt good to unwrap her toes and wiggle them.

She thought of the tryouts, just six weeks away. Maybe if she started practicing more, she could improve faster. She just had to start dancing better!

She noticed Pam and Lynn sitting near her and tried to ignore them.

"Are you going to the party Saturday?" Pam called over to her, as she and Lynn got up to leave.

The party was to be at Lynn's house, to celebrate the end of summer. Stacey had been invited, but she didn't want to go. She didn't want to tower over everyone. She'd feel like an oddball. Besides, she knew she'd only been asked because her brother Tommy and Lynn's brother were best friends. If Tommy was invited, Stacey would have to be, too.

"I'm not sure," she answered.

"A lot of boys will be there," Pam said. "Mark and some of the other guys from Ida May's classes are coming. It'll be a lot of fun."

She and Lynn turned to go, and Stacey heard them laughing as they went out the door. Suddenly she felt empty and left out.

Last year she and Pam had always left ballet class together. Now Pam and Lynn always left together and didn't even think about asking her to go with them.

Stacey packed her shoes in her carry-all bag and got up to leave. She knew why Pam had mentioned Mark. Mark, "the Tree," as he was called, was the tallest boy in the school—even taller than Stacey. Pam knew Stacey liked him.

Stacey sighed as she stepped outside into the bright September sun. She didn't know why she should go to the party just because Mark would be there. He hardly seemed to know she existed. He took ballet right before she did. But usually when she ran into him in the hall, he didn't even speak.

On the way home, she took a shortcut down an alley and then headed up Cimarron Street. Just as she was passing a yard on the corner of the alley, a voice called to her. "Deary, have you seen a little white fluffy dog?"

A short, roundish woman in gardening clothes came toward Stacey.

"Nope, sorry," Stacey said. "Haven't seen any dogs today."

The woman seemed puzzled as she looked up and down the alley. "What could have happened to that rascal? I'm house-sitting for my nephew, and my little dog Oscar doesn't know his way around yet. I wouldn't want him to get lost."

Stacey started to walk away, but the woman went on talking. "What's your name, deary?"

"Stacey."

The woman's blue eyes sparkled, and she looked ready to break out in laughter at any moment.

"Pleased to meet you, Stacey. I'm Mrs. Fremple." She moved her gardening trowel to her left hand and held out her right one. Then, seeing the dirt, she withdrew it and smiled. "Sorry, I forgot I'd been digging in the soil. My nephew doesn't like yard work much so I'm tidying up for him."

Stacey nodded politely, but all she really wanted to do was go home and sulk. Being tall was ruining her life!

"I see you have dancing slippers in your bag," Mrs. Fremple said. "You must be good at ballet, since you're so nice and tall."

Stacey frowned. What was so nice about being tall? This little woman didn't know much. "Well, not really," Stacey answered. "I've been taking lessons for seven years, but suddenly I feel like a telephone pole on toe shoes."

Mrs. Fremple's eyes sparkled and her mouth turned up in a friendly grin. "Mother nature has her ways, Stacey. Sometimes we don't know why but we turn out differently than other people. Take me for example.

What's taken off the top of me is spread around. My goodness, I look like a biscuit!"

Stacey wanted to laugh but didn't think it would be polite. Mrs. Fremple did look like the cute little dough boy on TV who laughed when his stomach was poked.

"Oscar! There you are!" Mrs. Fremple clapped her hands.

From up the alley, a little white fluffy dog with tail wagging ran at full speed toward Mrs. Fremple. She caught him in her arms and scratched his ears. "You know, I wanted to be a dancer once myself—a Spanish dancer. You know, the kind that click their heels and play the castinets and wear ruffled skirts?" She clicked her heels on the cement and did a quick spin around.

Picturing Mrs. Fremple in a ruffled skirt with a rose in her hair made Stacey laugh. "Why didn't you become a Spanish dancer?" she asked.

A smile lit up Mrs. Fremple's face. "It wasn't in the cards." Then she added in a whisper, "But sometimes when I'm alone I can't resist a quick twirl around the kitchen floor." She laughed. "Now I tear and stitch."

"What does that mean?" Stacey asked.

"I'm a seamstress. You know, I sew things. Tell your mother. Maybe she'll have me make you a dress or a costume."

"That's a good idea," Stacey said. "My mom doesn't like to sew much. I've been sewing the ribbons on my toe shoes for a long time now. It's hard pushing the needle through the material."

"Now tell me about your dancing. You must like it very much."

"Oh, yes I do—or I did. I don't think I'll ever be a real dancer now. Not with only legs and a neck."

"I'll tell you what to do," Mrs. Fremple said. "Come over some day and I'll take a few tucks in your knees. That will make you shorter." She winked.

"If it would work, I'd do it!" Stacey laughed.

Stacey felt a little better as she walked home. Maybe a person *could* be tall and still dance. Mrs. Fremple seemed to think so. But then Stacey's smile faded. There'd be only one part in the ballet for a tall person—the Nutcracker. And that was an undesirable part for anyone. The Nutcracker was a big, ugly giant. He didn't dance much, he just sort of ran around the stage. No, Stacey did not want to play the Nutcracker.

2
Oddball at the Party

Saturday was the day of the party, and Stacey tried hard to think up a good excuse not to go.

A half hour before it was to begin, Tommy knocked on her bedroom door. "Come on, Stace, we'll be late for the party."

"I'm not going," she answered through the closed door.

"You have to," he cried. "It's going to be neat."

"You don't need me," she said, "you have your own friends."

"Okay, but you don't know what you'll be missing. There'll be games and all kinds of food."

Stacey was silent.

"What'll I say when they see you're not with me?" Tommy asked.

"Tell them I'm not feeling well."

As soon as Tommy left for the party, Stacey came out of her room. She felt awful. She didn't like to lie and say she was sick, but she just couldn't bring herself to go to the party. Why should she go and stand out like a giraffe? And why should she go when she wasn't really wanted?

She looked out the front window. It was a beautiful, warm September day. Maybe a walk would help cheer her up. She headed out the door.

As she neared the corner, she saw a small, white fluffy dog running toward her, dragging a leash.

"Oscar!" she yelled. He wagged his tail and licked her hand with a wet tongue. "You do get around, don't you?"

Stacey scooped the dog up in her arms and patted his head. "I'd better take you home. Mrs. Fremple will be wondering where you are."

When she neared the alley, Mrs. Fremple appeared. Seeing Oscar and Stacey, she waved both arms. "Oh, you've found him! How delightful! And Stacey, I'm so happy to see you again." Mrs. Fremple's eyes shone.

Stacey felt warm inside. Somehow it was impossible to sulk for long around this little woman. It was almost as if she brought invisible magic dust with her and sprinkled it on Stacey's head.

"Isn't it a lovely day? Perfect weather to be outside having fun at a party."

"How did you know?"

"Know what?"

"About Lynn's party?"

Mrs. Fremple laughed. "Oh, deary, I've been invited to a garden party myself. Aren't the neighbors nice to include me? I'm so looking forward to it."

"I've been invited to a party, too," Stacey said. "But I'm not going."

"And why not?"

Stacey shrugged. "Don't know. Guess I feel out of place. You know, kind of bigger than everyone."

Mrs. Fremple looked startled. "Goodness, I'm bigger around than any of my neighbors. Maybe I should decide not to go to my party, either!"

"Oh, no, Mrs. Fremple, you have to go. You said you were looking forward to the party. Besides, you're an adult, so things are different for you."

"I'll tell you what," Mrs. Fremple said, her eyes twinkling. "I'll go to my party if you'll go to yours. If you won't go, neither will I!" Mrs. Fremple stamped her foot, but her eyes were twinkling. "I mean it, deary."

What could Stacey do? Somehow she knew Mrs. Fremple would keep her word. "All right, I'll go," she said reluctantly.

"Good! Now we can both have a good time." Mrs. Fremple waved as she walked away. Then she turned around and shouted, "Tell me all about your party later. Don't forget. I'll want a full report."

Now there was no getting out of it. Mrs. Fremple would ask her about the party and she'd have to have an answer. Well, she would just peek inside long enough to tell Mrs. Fremple she had gone.

Stacey sighed as she knocked on Lynn's front door.

Lynn's mother opened it. "Welcome to the party, Stacey."

Stacey forced a smile. Then she spotted Tommy in the distance, playing Ping-Pong with Mark.

"Hey, Amazon Woman!" Tommy shouted. "What are you doing here? I told them you were sick."

Stacey blushed. Brothers! She wanted to

shut him up but couldn't. "I'm feeling better."

"Good, you're here," Mark called out to her. "Now we can play basketball. Boys against the girls. I'll go get it started."

Stacey couldn't believe what she was hearing. Not only had Mark spoken to her, but he actually sounded glad to see her—even if it was just because she was good at basketball. Maybe the party wasn't going to be so bad, after all.

She followed Mark and Tommy outside. A bunch of girls from the ballet class were grouped around the pool, showing off the last of their summer tans. The girls were talking about *The Nutcracker* ballet.

"The music is fabulous," one of the girls said. "I can hardly wait until we learn some of the steps."

"What I can't wait for is to see who is going to be the Nutcracker," Pam said. Then she looked up. "Oh, hi, Stacey. Maybe you'll be it." She giggled.

Before Stacey could respond, Pam added, "It will have to be someone really tall, like you, to carry around that heavy head."

Stacey felt the heat rise up in her neck and face. She looked toward the basketball court to avoid having the girls see her blush. "Maybe Mark will do it." She saw him sink a basket easily over the heads of some other boys.

"Well," Pam said, "one of you probably will."

"Come on, Stacey, the girls need you," Tommy yelled from the court.

Of course Stacey knew the reason why. At least, being tall had one advantage. She was much closer to the basketball hoop than the rest of them.

She walked over to where they were playing.

"We're going to beat you guys," one of the girls shouted. "We've got Stacey!"

"Not if I can help it," Mark said. He bounced the ball in front of Stacey, then just as she was about to grab it, tossed it over her head and made a basket. Cheers went up from the boys.

Then Lynn got the ball and passed it to Stacey. Stacey took quick aim and sunk the ball to make a basket.

"Yea!" the girls cheered.

Stacey had to admit she was a pretty good basketball player. She and Tommy had practiced together in their backyard.

The game went on, with the lead shifting back and forth between the boys and the girls. But, in the end, the boys won.

Stacey didn't care. Playing basketball was fun. She'd even forgotten for a while how miserable it was to be tall. She wished they could play another game, but Lynn's mother brought the food out then. After that the girls went back to sitting around the pool, and the boys went back to playing Ping-Pong.

Stacey felt awkward and left out again. She finally went into the kitchen and visited with Lynn's mother. She was glad when eleven o'clock came and it was time to go.

The week after the party, whenever Mark would see her in the halls at school, he'd wave and say, "Hi, Ace."

It was nice having Mark pay attention to her. But Stacey wished he thought of her as a graceful ballerina rather than an ace basketball player.

3

Growing like a Weed

On Monday, Stacey was back in ballet class, trying some new steps.

"Elevate, Stacey," Ida May shouted. "Keep your knees straight and point your toes. Spring! Dance with the music!"

Stacey thought she was doing all those things. Her toes felt as if they were pushing right out of her shoes. When was Ida May going to give the class a rest? Stacey had been taking *pointe* lessons for a year, but she didn't know when her feet had hurt so much!

Ida May crouched at Stacey's feet and picked up her right leg. Then she waved it outward and put it back. "If you do the step with your leg like this, look what can happen." Ida May demonstrated the wrong stance and fell over. The class laughed.

"You may laugh now, but I don't think you'd laugh if this happened to you onstage.

Now girls, hold your heads up proudly, keep your eyes up, and relax. Dance as if you're flying across the Lincoln Center stage in New York. Once again now. Da-dum-de-dum...."

Stacey looked at herself and the others in the mirror. She was still a beat behind.

"Okay, break!" Ida May finally said with a clap of her hands. Then she took Stacey aside and asked in a low voice, "What's your trouble?"

Stacey looked away.

"You've been my student for a long time, Stacey. About seven years."

Stacey nodded.

"And you've been a good student. But lately you've been having trouble. Is there anything wrong?"

"I don't know," Stacey answered.

"If it's your growing, well, that's perfectly normal," Ida May told her. "You've sprouted up so fast that your muscles are having trouble supporting you. You're going to have to work harder to strengthen them and get used to your new form. But I know you can do it." Ida May smiled. "You've always been a hard worker."

Stacey appreciated Ida May's confidence in her. And she knew Ida May was right. She had been a hard worker, with almost perfect attendance. She'd missed only a few lessons for vacation.

"I know the steps, and I love to dance," Stacey mumbled. "Only lately I've felt as if I've been walking around with cans tied to my feet."

Ida May smiled. "I don't want you to worry. We'll work on the problem. Okay?"

Stacey nodded in agreement, but she was certain she couldn't work any harder than she was already.

"I hope you will try hard," Ida May said. "Tryouts will be five weeks from now. I'd like you to have a part in the ballet."

"Me too," Stacey said. "I want that more than anything."

"Good. I'll give you some dance exercises to practice at home."

Ida May walked over to the table and took a handful of papers. She gave one to Stacey, then handed the others out to the rest of the class.

Walking home from ballet class, Stacey saw Mrs. Fremple in her yard again. By her side was Oscar. He looked ready to run the hundred-yard dash at any second.

"Hello! Hello! Hello!" Mrs. Fremple called out. "How was your party? Mine was superb. I had a marvelous time. What did you do at your party?"

"We played basketball," Stacey answered.

"Basketball! I bet you're terrific at that sport!" Mrs. Fremple was kind enough not to say "because you're tall." Stacey was glad she didn't.

"How is your ballet coming along?"

"Okay," Stacey answered. "But not really. Tryouts for the recital are coming up in October, and I'm nervous about them. We're doing *The Nutcracker*, you know."

"Oh, when will that be?" Mrs. Fremple asked. "I won't want to miss it."

"Sometime in December. I'll let you know."

"Splendid! *The Nutcracker* is my favorite ballet. The costumes and the music are marvelous." Mrs. Fremple waved her trowel through the air as if it were a wand. "How naughty Clara's brother was to break her toy nutcracker!"

"How do you know so much about the ballet?" Stacey asked.

"I've made many costumes for dancers in my day," Mrs. Fremple explained.

"You have? You didn't tell me that," Stacey said. "You should let Ida May know."

"Is Ida May your teacher?"

"Yes, her studio is on Slauson Avenue."

"Well, maybe I'll just call on her. Now, tell me which part will you have? The Sugar Plum Fairy or perhaps the Snow Queen? Or maybe you'll be Clara?"

Stacey shook her head. "The way I've danced lately, I'll be lucky to be in the ballet."

"Oh my." Mrs. Fremple sighed. "Are you still having a problem?"

Stacey nodded. She hadn't meant to pour out her troubles again, but she didn't seem to have much control over her mouth right now. "Ever since this summer I've been growing like a weed. Then today, my teacher had a private talk with me. She wants me to work harder, but I'm not sure I can. I'm so tall I just can't seem to make my body do what it's supposed to."

"Tall, small. Do you think it's unjust to be tall?" Mrs. Fremple asked. "I'd really like to be taller, but there's nothing I can do about my height, is there? And look at old Oscar there. He'd probably like to be a Great Dane, but he'll never be."

Stacey smiled. She knew Mrs. Fremple was right. A person couldn't change being tall or small. Still, knowing that didn't make her feel any better.

Mrs. Fremple seemed to think a moment. "Maybe part of the trouble is that you need new ballet shoes."

"New shoes?"

"Well, yes. You said you've been growing

like a weed, so your feet must be growing, too."

Stacey looked down at her feet. "My toe shoes are so stretched out, I didn't think they could be too small. But maybe you're right. I'll go talk to Mom. Bye, Mrs. Fremple. I'll see you later."

At home, Stacey reported to her mother that she thought she needed new *pointe* shoes.

"I thought we just bought a pair," her mother said. "But then, I suppose you've grown since then." She sighed.

The next afternoon, Stacey and her mother went to the ballet supply store and picked out a new pair of pink satin toe shoes. They were a whole size larger than her old ones. And they felt better.

At home Stacey dutifully sewed the ribbons onto the sides of the new shoes. The satin was so smooth that she didn't like to poke holes into it, even though she knew one *pirouette* on a hardwood floor would make it look chewed up, anyway. Then she made a row of tiny embroidered stitches across each toe to help the material last longer.

When she'd finished sewing, she wrapped her toes carefully in lamb's wool, to keep blisters from forming. Then she put her new shoes on and wore them around the house to break them in. As she practiced stepping and turning, she hoped that the new shoes would help her do better. She was anxious to try them out in class.

After a thorough workout, she went to her room. She took off her shoes and dropped them on her bed. Then she sat down on the floor and rubbed the arches of her feet. She hummed the tune of the "Waltz of the Flowers" from *The Nutcracker* and thought about the tryouts, just five weeks away.

Maybe she would be chosen to play the part of a flower or a snowflake or one of the mice. No, she was too big and clumsy for those parts. Well, she'd be glad to play *any-thing*—except the big, ugly Nutcracker!

4

It's the Spirit That Counts!

During the next few weeks, Stacey worked hard. Her new shoes helped, or at least she thought they did. Ida May seemed preoccupied with the plans for the ballet and had stopped yelling at her.

Then, early in October, Ida May reminded the class that tryouts would be held the next week. "Please be in the auditorium of the junior high school by one o'clock. Can you all remember that?"

Mumbles of "yes" were heard around the room.

"Okay, see you there next week."

Stacey spent every spare moment of the week practicing all the steps she'd learned. She jumped, leaped, and pirouetted around the house.

On Saturday morning, Stacey woke up early with a bad case of the butterflies. It was the day of the tryouts, and even though she told herself there was nothing to be nervous about, she was. She put on her practice leotard and went downstairs. She'd hoped no one would be up yet, but Tommy was already in the living room, watching cartoons on television. Stacey twirled past him.

"Get out of the way," he told her.

"This is more important than television," she said.

"Maybe it is to you, but not to me," he said.

"I'm going to be a dancer on television someday," Stacey said, turning in front of him.

"Huh," Tommy grunted, his eyes glued to the TV screen.

Stacey ignored him and stretched out her legs. Using the back of a chair for a *barre*, she lifted one leg up onto it. Then she bent over and touched her forehead to her knees. After that, she did a series of backbends to loosen up her back muscles. All during her exercises, she kept checking the clock. The morning was going so slowly!

When she'd finished limbering up, she practiced some of the combinations she'd been working on. Finally she felt she was as ready as she would ever be. She went upstairs and packed her carry-all bag, putting in her shoes and lamb's wool.

She decided to wear her black leotard to make herself look smaller. She put on a skirt over her tights. She wound her hair into a tight bun at the top of her head and tucked several pins in to hold the bun in place. Then she put on a hairnet and sprayed her hair with hairspray. She didn't want her hair to topple down when she jumped.

At last the clock said twelve-thirty. Stacey couldn't stand to wait any longer and decided to go. School was only a fifteen minute walk, but it was better to be early than late.

"See you later, Mom," she called through the house.

"Do you want a ride?" her mother's voice echoed back.

"No. I'll walk. I have enough time. Keep your fingers crossed for me."

Stacey cut down the alley and then through the park. It was the usual route she took to school. But on this day she met Mrs. Fremple, walking Oscar.

"Hello, there. Off to dancing, are you?" she asked. "You look just like a ballerina today, with your hair in a bun like that."

"Thanks," Stacey said. "I hope I do. Today we're having auditions for the recital. Keep your fingers crossed that I get a part."

"Luck and magic aren't what you need," Mrs. Fremple said. "It's the spirit that counts!" Then quite suddenly, right there in the middle of the park, Mrs. Fremple clicked her heels, clapped her hands, and spun around like a Spanish dancer. "Without spirit, a dancer can never be great!" She stopped dancing and looked around. "Where did Oscar go?"

"Over there, I think," Stacey said.

"Right. Oh, I see him now. Toodle-doo, deary. And remember, it's the spirit that counts."

What in the world was Mrs. Fremple

talking about? Funny old lady, dancing that way. And she didn't even seem embarrassed.

Stacey walked on. When she arrived at the auditorium, the auditions were already underway. At first she thought she was late. Then she realized that Ida May's baby class was trying out first.

Pam and Lynn were in the front of the auditorium, warming up. Stacey sat down near them. They looked like twins. Both of them had their hair tied in buns on top of their heads. They were wearing matching red leotards with green hose. They looked like Tweedle-dee and Tweedle-dum at Christmastime, Stacey thought. Well, her black leotard wasn't very lively, but at least it made her look smaller.

It was nearing one o'clock. Stacey's class would be next. She took her shoes out of her bag and put them on. Then she took off her skirt and began doing warm-up exercises.

Behind her, she heard Lynn whisper, "Poor Mark."

She turned around. Lynn and Pam were both looking toward the side of the auditorium. Mark was standing there, gym bag in hand. He looked like he would rather be anyplace else.

"What happened to him?" Stacey asked.

"He's going to be the Nutcracker," Pam said.

"How do you know that?" Stacey asked, not quite believing what she had heard.

"Ida May made the announcement just before you got here."

Stacey could hardly contain herself! Now she wouldn't have to worry about getting the part anymore. Mark was a natural for it. He was tall and had broad shoulders. He could carry the big head of the Nutcracker easily.

Besides that, Stacey felt glad that Pam and Lynn had included her in their conversation.

The baby class left the stage. Ida May stepped over the footlights and looked out at the audience. "Friday's class on stage!"

"That's us!" Pam said.

Stacey followed the rest of the girls up the side stairs leading to the stage. Everyone lined up. Pam and Lynn got in the front row right under Ida May's nose.

Stacey stood in the back of the group and faced the footlights. There was something exciting about dancing on stage in front of lights. It was different from dancing in front of a mirror. The glow from the lights kept you from seeing the audience. Yet, there was a feeling of excitement that came from knowing people were watching.

The girls around her fidgeted and giggled nervously.

Ida May called out the combination of steps. The routine included leaps and finished with a *pique en arabesque.*

Stacey listened closely, trying to memorize the combination and to put all the steps together in her mind.

"Ready an-nd," Ida May said, nodding toward the piano player.

The music began. Stacey could see over the heads of the other girls. They were all about the same size. Counting to herself, she stepped out on *pointe*, jumped, and turned. She smiled, thinking she had done the routine fairly well.

But Ida May frowned. "You can all do better than that!" she said. "There's no need to be nervous now. This isn't opening night. This is just a practice. Now, take it from the top!"

Stacey retied the ribbons on her ankles. Then she stretched her legs and shook them to loosen them up. She breathed deeply and waited for the music to begin.

All the while she heard Mrs. Fremple's words, "It's the spirit that counts!" She wasn't sure what Mrs. Fremple had meant, but she did know she loved dancing and when all the steps worked together, she felt good.

The music started again. Stacey tried to stick with the beat. Right foot, left foot. The steps worked better for her this time. Although she was nervous, she put everything she had into the routine.

When she stopped, she let out a sigh. Suddenly she realized she had been holding her breath. That wasn't being very relaxed! She breathed deeply while Ida May checked her list of names.

Using a pencil for a pointer, Ida May pointed to each girl and called off the names. "Sandra, Claryce, Elise, Bunny, Susan, Mary, Karen, Pam, and Lynn—over here. Stacey—on the other end, please."

Ida May was lining up everyone according to height.

"Now then," Ida May said, "do this for me. Step turn, step turn, step back, step front, *assemblé, assemblé, pirouette,* and run, run, run. Got it?" Ida May demonstrated the pattern she wanted the girls to do.

Stacey listened and watched carefully.

"On three," Ida May counted. "One, two, three!" Her hand came down to show when the girls were supposed to start.

Stacey concentrated on the steps. This was not the time to think about sore toes, blisters, or aching muscles.

"One, two, three, FOUR!" Ida May put the emphasis on the last beat.

When the girls had finished, Ida May didn't

say anything. She wrote some notes on her clipboard, then looked up.

"Because most of you are the same size, I'd like you to be in the *corps de ballet*, or chorus. Some of you will be Flowers, some Snowflakes, and some Mice."

"Who will be the Snow Queen and the Sugar Plum Fairy?" someone asked.

"Most of the solo roles will be danced by the advanced students. But as the *corps*, you will do a lot of dancing and be on stage a lot of the time."

Various sounds broke out of, "oh, boy," and "super." But Stacey was silent. Somehow she didn't feel excited.

"I'll put the rehearsal schedule up next week," Ida May said. "Okay, that's all —except for Stacey." She turned to her. "Will you stay a moment?"

Stacey had suspected all along that she was too tall to fit in with the chorus. Was Ida May going to tell her that she did not get to dance in the ballet at all?

After the stage was clear, Ida May said,

"Thank you for staying. Will you try a few steps for me?"

"By myself?"

"If you would, please."

Stacey was puzzled. Was she going to be in the *corps*, or wasn't she? Ida May had already said the solo parts would be danced by the advanced students. So Stacey obviously was not going to get a leading role. She would have been surprised if she did.

"*Pirouettes* upstage to stage right, please."

Stacey got into position. She put her feet in fourth position and curved her arms in front of her. Ida May stood behind her and pushed her chin up. "Ready?"

"Yes," Stacey answered. She held her head high and kept her eyes straight ahead.

"Good. Begin."

Stacey twirled to stage right, keeping her eyes on the red velvet curtains so that she wouldn't get dizzy. When she'd finished, Ida May put her arm around Stacey's shoulder and looked her in the eyes. "I've noticed a remarkable improvement in your dancing,

Stacey, and I'd like to try something special with you."

Stacey could hear her heart thump as Ida May spoke to her. What was she going to say?

"As you know, it's important to have understudies for each major role, just in case something should happen to the dancer. I'd like you to understudy for Maria Stark. She's a dancer from Jay Lanova's Studio. She will be dancing the part of the Sugar Plum Fairy."

The bottom suddenly dropped out of Stacey's stomach. The understudy! That was like no role at all. Nothing ever happened to the leading dancers. Even if they were sick, they always showed up to dance their parts.

Ida May kept talking, but Stacey didn't hear her. She knew that being an understudy was supposed to be an honor, yet she couldn't help feeling left out—as though she wasn't going to be part of the ballet, at all.

Stacey looked away. She didn't want her eyes to give away the disappointment she was feeling. She had to fight to hold back her tears.

Forcing a smile she said, "Good." But being an understudy didn't seem like something special.

How could she face her dance class? They'd all be working hard together to learn the dances for the chorus, and she'd be off in a corner somewhere, doing nothing.

"Then it's all set," Ida May said. "I'll let you know the rehearsal schedule."

Stacey left the stage. The auditorium was empty except for Pam and Lynn in the back. They had probably hung around to see what part she got. Stacey sat down in the front row and tried to avoid them. As she started to remove her shoes, the tears she had tried to hold back formed in her eyes.

"Well, what did she say?" Pam asked, rushing up to her. "What part did you get?"

"None," Stacey said quietly, turning her head. She didn't want Pam or Lynn to see her cry. "I'm going to understudy for the Sugar Plum Fairy."

There was a moment of silence. Stacey could tell exactly what Pam and Lynn were thinking, without even looking at them.

Finally Pam said, "Oh! How nice. Well, at least it's something. Come on, Lynn. See you at practice, Stacey." She called over her shoulder as she and Lynn headed up the aisle.

Stacey watched them leave. She was hurt by Pam's coldness, and she felt left out. Pam and Lynn could have invited her to go with them. But they didn't. Now Stacey would be even more of an outcast. Being an understudy would automatically put her on a different practice schedule than the others in her regular class.

Stacey took her ballet shoes off and was slipping her skirt over her leotard when Mark walked up.

"I saw you dance," he said. "You were really good."

"Oh, hi, Mark!" she said, surprised but pleased that he had noticed her. "Thanks. Only it didn't get me very far. I'm going to be an understudy."

"Don't feel bad," he said. "I'm going to be the Nutcracker."

"I heard," Stacey said sympathetically.

"Guess there's no one taller than the 'Tree.'" Mark grinned.

Stacey looked him in the eyes. "You'll be perfect for the part. Congratulations!"

"At least I can hide under the big head of the Nutcracker and no one will see me." Mark laughed.

Stacey laughed, too. "You're just lucky to be in the ballet. I wish I could be."

"But you have an important part," Mark said. "You should feel honored to be an understudy for a leading role."

Stacey felt a little better. Mark was being nice. He hadn't laughed at her or put her down in any way. And he was a good sport about his own role.

Stacey and Mark left the auditorium together. Once outside, he hopped on his bicycle. "I've got papers to deliver," he said. "I'll see you later."

"See you at school!" Stacey called after him. She watched him ride off and thought how nice it would be to be his friend.

Walking home, Stacey wondered just what being an understudy would mean. What would her mother say? All those lessons for nothing. And Tommy would probably have a wonderful time teasing her now. What was more terrible, Pam and Lynn were probably gloating over their part in the *corps de ballet* right now.

Nothing seemed fair anymore!

Nearing home, Stacey was stopped by Oscar, jumping up and down and barking at her legs. Of course, right behind him was Mrs. Fremple.

"Good afternoon, Stacey," she said. "Oh, no, I can see it's not good. Are you hurt?"

Stacey couldn't hold back the tears any longer. They poured out.

"Oh, my," Mrs. Fremple said. "There's not a cloud in the sky, but it seems to be raining." She put her arm around Stacey and led her to a bench. "Now tell Fremple all about it."

Stacey pulled a Kleenex from her ballet bag and dabbed at her eyes. "I didn't get a part in the ballet . . . not even in the chorus. I

56

danced with spirit, like you said, but all I got out of it was being picked to be understudy for the Sugar Plum Fairy."

Mrs. Fremple didn't say anything.

"I know it's because I'm just too big. I don't fit in anywhere." Stacey sobbed.

"Well," Mrs. Fremple said, "you can feel sorry for yourself if you like, but I really don't know why you should. It seems to me you have an important job ahead of you, just to learn the Sugar Plum Fairy part. I'd say you were on your way to becoming a solo performer. If you do well as an understudy, you should stand a good chance of getting the Sugar Plum Fairy part next year."

"Do you really think so?" Stacey asked. "I hadn't thought of the understudy part that way. I won't be on stage at all during the performance. I'll be letting my mom down, and the other kids will think I didn't get a part because I'm a terrible dancer."

"So what do you want to do—quit?"

Stacey thought about Mrs. Fremple's question. Could she really give up dancing after seven years?

"No," she answered firmly. "I could never do that."

"I'm sure your mother will understand."

"But she's spent so much money on my lessons for so many years, I can't believe she won't be disappointed," Stacey said.

"Why don't you try her and see?"

"Well, okay," Stacey said, forcing a smile. "I hope you're right."

She said goodbye to Mrs. Fremple and walked the rest of the way home, hugging her carry-all bag to her for comfort. She wasn't at all eager to tell her mother the news. But she would have to, sooner or later.

Her mother was in the kitchen putting away the groceries when Stacey walked in. "Stacey, you're home! How did it go?"

"I didn't get a part," Stacey mumbled. A tear rolled from her eye and fell onto the back of her hand.

"Nothing at all?"

"Nothing very good," Stacey said. "I'm

only an understudy." She waited for her mother's reaction.

"Understudy for what?"

Stacey knew she'd let her mother down after all the years of lessons. "Ida May wants me to learn the part of the Sugar Plum Fairy."

Stacey's mother laughed. "Stacey, I can see a wonderful opportunity here for you to learn a lot. And who knows what might happen? You may actually get to dance during the performance. This is your growing time, your learning time."

"She's growing all right," Tommy interrupted. "Right through the roof!"

"That's enough, Tommy," her mother said. She turned to Stacey. "It takes a lot of help to put on a good show. I'm sure Ida May is counting on you. I know you'll do whatever you can to assist her."

Stacey nodded. "Yeah, I guess, but I sure wish I was really in the show!"

5

Heads Up!

The rehearsal schedule was posted at the next class. Stacey found her name at the bottom of the list, next to Maria Stark's. Their practice time was the same as for the *corps de ballet*. Stacey frowned. Now everyone would know that she wasn't really in the ballet.

She waited for Pam and Lynn to go into their practice room before she went into her smaller one at the end of the hall. Maria hadn't arrived yet. Stacey covered her toes with lamb's wool and slipped into her *pointe* shoes. Then she went to the *barre* to warm up.

In a short time, a girl who looked about college age came in. "Hi! I'm Maria Stark," the girl said, her dark eyes shining. "You must be Stacey. Ida May said you'd be here today. We're to work on the Sugar Plum Fairy part together."

"I know," Stacey said, not knowing what else to say. Standing flat-footed next to Maria, Stacey was overjoyed to see they were both the same height. What a relief! She wouldn't have to stoop over to talk with her.

"Ida May will help us soon, but right now she's working in the other room with the *corps de ballet*," Maria said. "We're on our own for a while." She smiled.

Maria wasn't very pretty, but she was nice and had the straightest back Stacey had ever seen.

"I like to deep-breathe before starting, don't you?" Maria asked.

Stacey nodded, though she wasn't used to doing deep-breathing exercises as part of her warm-up routine.

Maria sucked in some air and let it out slowly. She put her hands on her rib cage and said, "From here. Pull up your shoulders, hold your back and head high. Now let the air out slowly."

61

Stacey imitated Maria. But as she let the air out, her normal slouch returned.

"Don't deflate yourself," Maria said. "You're not a balloon. Breathe out, but keep your body up. Dancers learn to conserve energy. Let the air go, nice and easy. Don't exaggerate the motions of breathing."

Stacey tried to follow Maria's instructions and felt good doing the exercise.

"You know, we're really lucky, you and I," Maria said.

"What do you mean?"

"Being tall. Tall people have a lot to show off, and they should do it proudly. Look at Juliet Prowse. She's very tall and a beautiful dancer."

Maria started doing a stretching exercise, and Stacey followed her. She felt herself stretching taller and taller as they twirled and stepped and moved their arms over their heads and around their bodies. The exercise felt wonderful! Now Stacey knew she was ready to learn the dance of the Sugar Plum Fairy.

"Watch me," Maria said, "and tell me what I'm doing wrong. I seem to miss a count somewhere in this routine." She moved her feet into a jump, changed their position in the air, landed, sprang up again, landed, and raised up onto her toes. She counted as she danced, "One and two and three and oops! I lost four. You do the combination for me, please."

Stacey tried it and was surprised that it worked out right.

"I see now," Maria commented. "I need that added lift that you give your jumps. Good. Now watch and see if I do the combination right!"

Stacey beamed. Imagine Maria asking *her* what she was doing wrong and how to do the combination! Stacey liked working with Maria.

When Ida May returned, she focused her attention on Stacey. She moved her arms until they were in the right position, tilted Stacey's chin, moved her head to one side. When Stacey didn't get a step, Ida May worked

63

with her patiently, repeating the directions. Stacey felt she was getting special treatment.

"Maria, run through this for me," Ida May said. "And, Stacey, you stay right beside her."

Stacey had never worked this hard at dancing before.

As the days went on, she felt her legs grow stronger, and she became more sure of herself.

"Heads up!" Ida May would say to Maria and Stacey, and they'd look at each other and laugh. It was a private secret between them. "Heads up" was one of Ida May's favorite expressions.

Rehearsal and practice took every bit of Stacey's extra time, and she didn't see Mrs. Fremple for weeks. Every time she walked by Mrs. Fremple's yard, she wasn't home, or wasn't in her garden. And Stacey didn't walk through the park anymore. Now that the days were getting shorter, her mother picked her up in the car from Ida May's studio.

Then one day, after practice, Ida May said, "Costume fittings begin next week. Stacey, your fitting is on Tuesday."

"Does that mean I get a costume, too?" she asked excitedly.

Ida May shook her head. "You'll only be measured. If Maria can't make all the performances, her costume will be altered to fit you. You're close to being the same size, so there shouldn't be much of a problem."

At school on Tuesday, Pam ran into Stacey in the hall. She told her all about the costumes for the *corps de ballet.* "We wear gorgeous snowflake costumes with white satin bodices and silver glitter all over the skirts. Then for the last act, we change into pastel-colored tutus that make us look like spring flowers."

Stacey tried hard not to be envious, though she longed to wear a costume of her own. "I'm having my fitting today at 3:15," she said.

Pam didn't seem to hear her. "Be glad you're not in the *corps de ballet.* It's *so* hard. We have all these different parts to learn. And Ida May gets really mad when someone is off beat. We have to stay together, you know."

The only thing Stacey could think of to say was "I'm learning a lot from Maria."

"Well," Pam said, with her nose a little in the air, "the *corps de ballet* is the most important part of the show. So we have to work extra hard. See you later."

Stacey wondered if Pam realized that the *corps* was not the most important part of the show. The ballet wouldn't be as beautiful or exciting without the Sugar Plum Fairy or the Prince. And there'd be no ballet without the Nutcracker. But Stacey didn't say anything. She watched Pam walk away.

Stacey was prompt for her fitting. She arrived at Ida May's studio at 3:15 and was surprised to find Mrs. Fremple there.

"What are you doing here?" Stacey asked.

"Hi, deary. I took your suggestion and asked Ida May if she needed help with costumes and, well, here I am. Haven't seen you around lately to tell you the news."

"Rehearsals have kept me busy," Stacey told her.

"Ah, yes. And I see I'm to measure you for the Sugar Plum Fairy costume. Would you like to see it?"

"Oh, yes," Stacey said, enthusiastically.

Mrs. Fremple shuffled through a rack of net skirts until she found a bright pink tutu. She handed it to Stacey. "Why don't you just slip into it so I can see what changes need to be made for you."

"It's a lovely color," Stacey said.

"Mind the pins," Mrs. Fremple warned her. "One good stick and you'll leap like a frog!"

Stacey stood in front of the mirror and admired the way the dress looked on her. What fun it would be to dance in it!

"There now, it fits practically like it was made for you," Mrs. Fremple said. "And you never know, it might be yours to wear."

"Oh, no. I wouldn't want anything terrible to happen to Maria. She's a good friend and a great dancer. I couldn't ever do as well as she," Stacey said, stepping out of the dress. "But it is pretty, and I'm glad I got to try it on."

"It's such fun sewing costumes again," Mrs. Fremple said with a smile. "I love all the glitter and bright colors that go with a show."

Stacey got dressed and then looked over the rack of unfinished costumes. "You're making all of these?"

"No, no. I'm just a helper," Mrs. Fremple told her. "But I'd like to wear them." Mrs. Fremple snapped her fingers and twirled around again like a Spanish dancer.

Stacey held up a bright blue pair of trousers piped in yellow. "Who are these for?"

"Oh, those are for the Nutcracker. There'll be a crimson red jacket to go with them and, of course, the big papier-mâché head. Most attractive, don't you think?"

"Yes," Stacey said. "No one will know Mark is under all that."

6

Part of the Show

Practice sessions for the ballet changed into rehearsals. All the classes moved from Ida May's studio onto the stage of the school auditorium. There were many times when the whole cast worked together and other times when they worked separately.

Stacey attended the same rehearsals as Maria and the *corps de ballet,* only she didn't get to dance. She sat in the audience and watched. She watched the *corps de ballet* go over their dances as dancing mice, swirling snowflakes, and prancing flowers. She watched Maria and the Snow Queen and the Russian dancers and the Gingerbread men. And she danced along with each part in her head. She did so much watching, she was certain she could understudy anyone's part, but she still felt left out.

Finally, Ida May called her, "Stacey, Stacey, where are you?" Ida May hung over the footlights on the stage and searched the audience.

"Here!" Stacey waved her arms from where she sat in the middle of the auditorium.

"Run through your number with Maria, will you?"

Stacey jumped up. Would she? She'd been ready for hours! She only hoped she wasn't too stiff from sitting.

On stage, Maria was doing stretching exercises. Stacey joined her, loosening her back, arms, and legs. They did a few practice turns and jumps, then Maria started her deep-breathing exercise. Stacey breathed deeply, too, but felt silly doing it. Especially when she saw Pam and Lynn in the wings with their heads together.

"Whenever you're ready," Ida May said.

"I'm ready," Maria said.

"All right. Heads up!" Ida May brought her hand down to start the music and the dancers.

Stacey knew the dance by heart. She stayed far enough away from Maria to give her plenty of room.

When the dance was finished, Ida May said, "Stacey, please do it alone."

Stacey's heart sank. Had she made a mistake?

Maria smiled at her and gave her a nod of confidence.

"Center stage, Stacey," Ida May told her.

Red and blue footlights shone in Stacey's face. She felt self-conscious and nervous, alone on the open stage.

"Whenever you're ready," Ida May said.

Stacey glanced toward Maria, who smiled at her again. "Ready," Stacey said, pulling herself up as straight as she could.

The music began. As soon as Stacey started to dance, all of her fear and tension vanished. Her feet moved automatically, as if programmed by a computer. Having the whole stage to herself gave her a wonderfully free feeling. If only the moment would never end!

When she had finished the dance, Maria applauded and said, "Bravo!"

Stacey hoped that Pam and Lynn were watching. But the auditorium was empty except for Ida May and Maria. And for Mark, who was just coming in.

"Thank you," Ida May said. "That was the best I've seen you dance. Keep that up and next year, you will be the Sugar Plum Fairy!"

Stacey gulped. Was Mrs. Fremple right? Had Ida May picked her as understudy so she could train for the part for next year? It looked that way. Ida May didn't say things she didn't mean. Maybe all the hard work had been worth it, after all.

Ida May turned toward the side of the auditorium, where Mark was.

"You're late!" Ida May snapped.

"Couldn't help it. We had a basketball game."

"Well, don't be late again. Luckily there's not much dancing to your part. Clara will guide you around by the hand. Now where's Clara?"

"She isn't here yet," Stacey said. The part of Clara was being played by a girl from Jay Lanova's studio.

"Well, then, Stacey," Ida May said, "you're our faithful stand-in. Would you play Clara for now?"

"What do I do?"

"Just take the Nutcracker by the hand and lead him around to the X mark on the center stage. Mark, go offstage. Clara will come and take your hand."

Stacey clopped across the stage on the flat part of her toe shoes. They were not made for walking.

As the music began, she hesitated to take Mark's hand. She didn't want to seem forward. But Mark took her hand first and didn't seem to mind at all.

As they neared the X mark on the stage, Mark said, "Hey, let's polka!" He turned Stacey around in a circle and they skipped a few steps across the floor.

"This is fun!" she said quietly. She knew the part did not call for dancing, and Ida May was sure to stop them at any minute.

And Ida May did. "You won't be able to dance that much when you're wearing the big head," she told Mark, "but you can twirl a few times."

Stacey and Mark rehearsed his part all the way through twice. The girl who was playing Clara showed up just when Mark had to leave.

"Sorry, I have a paper route to take care of," Mark said.

Ida May sighed, shook her head, then excused him with a wave of her hand. "Go ahead, but don't forget what you've learned today."

Mark nodded and left the stage.

"There'll be a dress rehearsal with the whole cast the week before the performance," Ida May called after him. "You must be here for it."

"I will be. Don't worry." Mark's voice echoed from the audience.

Ida May turned to face Stacey. "Well, it looks like you'll have to take Mark's place now and show Clara what to do. My goodness, Stacey, you're turning into the most valuable member of the cast."

Stacey felt a surge of pride. Ida May made her feel important. She was part of the show whether or not the audience would ever see her. Maybe being the star was not as important as she'd thought. It was fun to be an understudy and learn everyone's part. She stretched up as tall as she could and walked through Mark's part with the girl playing Clara.

7

Standing Straight and Tall

Dress rehearsal was held the week before the performance. Again, Stacey sat in the audience and watched the whole show. The stage was like a fairyland with the lights on. The costumes and sets sparkled magically.

Stacey felt relaxed, since she wasn't actually performing. Yet she also felt a part of the show. Wherever she was needed, she helped out. She even pushed racks of costumes into the dressing rooms for Mrs. Fremple.

"The costumes are beautiful," she told Mrs. Fremple. Now and then she still felt a twinge of disappointment that she couldn't wear one, but she had decided that she might as well get used to the idea.

78

Then on Saturday morning, the day of opening night, Stacey was awakened by the phone ringing. She could hear her mother talking, and it sounded as if something was wrong.

"I see. Yes, I see," her mother kept repeating.

Sensing trouble, Stacey got up and walked out into the hall.

"Here she is now," her mother said. She called to Stacey, "It's Ida May. Please talk to her."

Stacey took the phone from her mother.

"We have an emergency," Ida May said. "Could you meet me at the auditorium in an hour?"

Stacey heard what Ida May said but didn't really understand. Was something wrong with Maria? Was she going to get a chance to dance the part of the Sugar Plum Fairy after all?

"What's the matter?" she asked expectantly.

"Mark twisted his ankle while playing basketball and we need to replace him."

Still partially asleep, Stacey wondered what that had to do with her.

Ida May went on, "We need you to take Mark's place as the Nutcracker!"

Stacey almost dropped the receiver. Was this really happening? Was what she feared most coming true? "I can't be the Nutcracker!" she cried. "I'm understudy for the Sugar Plum Fairy!"

"Yes, I know that, Stacey," Ida May said. "But you practically know the part already, and you're a fast learner. We need you."

Stacey thought about Pam and Lynn. Boy, would they have a good laugh over this! And Tommy would have enough ammunition to last a lifetime. Instead of calling her "Amazon Woman," he'd call her the "Nutcracker"!

"I don't really want to do it," Stacey said. She knew she was being selfish. How could she let Ida May down after all the special treatment she'd been given? She didn't like the way her selfishness made her feel.

She sighed and added in a low voice, "But I will."

"Stacey, you're a real trooper," Ida May said. "Don't let anyone say you're not! And

80

please try to get here as soon as you can!"

As Stacey hung up the phone, Tommy was just coming into the hall. "So what's up?" he asked.

"Nothing," she said and turned to her mother. "Oh, Mom, I don't want to be the ugly old Nutcracker. I want to be a ballerina. The Nutcracker barely dances and with that head on I'll look taller than ever!"

Tommy laughed. "You? The Nutcracker? That's great! I thought it was going to be Mark!"

"It was," she answered flatly. "He twisted his ankle playing basketball."

"Well, don't worry, no one will know it's you inside that head. They'll just think it's Mark."

"You can do a good job, Stacey," her mother encouraged her. "And you might even have fun playing the Nutcracker."

Stacey let her mother's and her brother's words sink in for a minute. Maybe she *could* have fun being the Nutcracker. Especially if no one knew it was she instead of Mark inside the costume. And being tall, she could pass for Mark easily.

"Okay, I'll do it," she said, and ran to get dressed.

She put on a pair of blue jeans and a shirt. Then she hurried off to the auditorium.

When she got there, Ida May ran over to her and grabbed her hand. "One thing about show business," Ida May said, "you have to be ready for the unexpected. You never know what's going to happen."

Stacey tried to be cheerful, but she felt nervous. She hoped they could finish the practice session before the rest of the cast arrived.

"The first thing you should do is have Mrs. Fremple alter the costume. You'll find her in dressing room B."

Stacey went backstage. She found Mrs. Fremple sitting in a chair, sewing sequins onto a satin bodice. "Oh, there you are! Come in and try these trousers on for me."

"I don't really want to play the part of the Nutcracker, you know."

"Ah, but you'll do it with spirit, and you'll do it well!"

Stacey slipped into the trousers and turned away from the mirror while Mrs. Fremple put pins in the proper places. Stacey didn't look in the mirror. She didn't want to see herself in the giant's costume.

When the costume had been pinned to fit her, Mrs. Fremple got the Nutcracker head from a table and brought it to Stacey. It was brightly painted and had a big mouth and heavy, black eyebrows.

"Oh, it's so ugly," Stacey said.

"Here, put it on, Deary. You'll need to practice walking around with it on. It's heavy."

The head rested on Stacey's shoulders. "Please, Mrs. Fremple," Stacey mumbled through the papier-mâché head. "Don't tell anyone I'm inside."

"Your secret is safe with me," Mrs. Fremple said. "Now go practice so that I can do more work. I'll sew up your costume after you finish practicing!"

Stacey returned to the stage to rehearse with the girl who was playing Clara. They were the only two people present, except for Ida May. The other dancers had the day off to relax before the recital.

"All right now, Clara, take the hand of the Nutcracker and bring him onto the stage," Ida May directed.

Stacey peeked through the eyeholes and followed Clara to the X mark on the stage. She moved carefully so she would not get stuck by the pins that Mrs. Fremple had put in the costume.

The two of them walked through the Nutcracker's part for a couple of hours, until Ida May was satisfied.

Stacey was anxious to get out of the big head. It was heavy and hot under it. She was just beginning to remove it when she saw Pam and Lynn coming onto the stage. She quickly put it back on. She didn't want them to see her.

"Ida May," Pam called out, walking right past Stacey. "Lynn and I want to try on our snowflake costumes again. We think they're mixed up and if we switched they'd fit better."

Ida May nodded. "Yes, go ahead. Mrs. Fremple is back in room B."

Pam and Lynn passed by Stacey and stopped. Lynn knocked on the head. "Knock, knock, who's there?"

Stacey froze. Did they know?

Then Pam said, "Hi, Mark! How is it inside?"

Stacey nodded but said nothing. Pam and Lynn went away laughing. Inside the head, Stacey was laughing, too. She'd fooled them. Maybe this was going to be kind of fun.

Ida May came over to her. "Stacey, you're terrific. Thanks for stepping in so graciously to help out at the last minute."

"You're welcome," Stacey answered and meant it.

When Pam and Lynn were backstage, Stacey was able to get out of the head and costume and sneak out of the auditorium. She skipped home to rest before the performance.

At dinner that night Stacey didn't want to eat too much because she was a little excited.

"Whenever you're ready, I'll drive you to school," her mother said when they'd finished eating.

"I'm ready now," Stacey said. She knew if she timed it right, she could sneak in while the other girls were putting on their make-up.

She didn't have any need for her toe shoes or lamb's wool, but she took them anyway. It would be terrible if something happened to Maria at the last minute and she wasn't prepared to walk on for her.

"I'll come backstage after the performance," Stacey's mother said.

"Good. Bring Tommy, too!"

"Don't worry. You know how he likes to tag along. And, Stacey, enjoy yourself."

"I will. Thanks. Bye, Mom." Stacey got out of the car and ran toward the stage door.

She walked in quietly and looked around. There were noises and laughter coming from the make-up room. Good. She was just in time.

She went quickly to the costume room and found the Nutcracker's outfit. Then she took it to another room to change. No one was around. Not even Mrs. Fremple or Ida May. She had timed her arrival just right.

After dressing quickly, Stacey stowed her street clothes in a corner and walked to the wings to wait for the show to begin.

There was lots of chatter backstage. Girls passing her couldn't resist tapping the big Nutcracker head and making some kind of remark.

"Hi, Mark!"

"Hello in there!"

Through it all, Stacey laughed to herself and nodded the big Nutcracker head.

Then at eight o'clock, the curtain went up. Ida May had lined everyone up and given them their cues for entering the stage. A recording of the overture for the ballet started playing over the stereo loudspeaker system.

Stacey felt the lovely melody run through her whole body, and her feet itched to dance. If only she could let loose and dance to the music instead of plodding along like some giant!

She watched the opening scene through the eyeholes of the giant-sized head.

Clara's brother threw the nutcracker toy on the floor and smashed it. Then when everyone was in bed, Clara returned to the living room to find the broken nutcracker.

Stacey tensed up. Any second now she would make her appearance. As soon as Clara started to cry, Ida May gave Stacey a gentle push.

"Good luck, Mark," Pam whispered.

Stacey smiled to herself as she stepped onstage into the bright spotlight. Through the eyeholes of her mask, she could glimpse the brilliant red and blue colors of her costume. What a good job Mrs. Fremple had done! The costume looked great.

People applauded when Clara brought the Nutcracker to the center of the stage.

It didn't take Stacey long to get into the part. She was a big character, and she acted like one. Instead of plodding along, she swayed to the music in a kind of half-dance, half-walk. She hammed up the part whenever she could. At the end of the scene, Stacey could hear loud applause.

Later, during the intermission, she was dying to remove the head and get some air. But she wouldn't do it around Pam or Lynn. She didn't need to be laughed at.

"You're doing great! Just great!" Ida May told her. "Why don't you take off that head and get a drink of water."

"No thanks," Stacey mumbled. "I might not be able to get it back on again."

But pretty soon she couldn't stand it any longer. After making sure Pam and Lynn were at the far side of the stage, she stepped into the shadows and loosened the mask. She took a few deep breaths of air and a drink of water, then put the head on firmly again.

Ida May called in a loud whisper, "Places everyone!"

Gingerbread men, Mice, Snowflakes, and Flowers began lining up in the wings. Stacey saw Maria, dressed in the bright pink costume of the Sugar Plum Fairy. "Good luck," she mumbled through the mask.

"Stacey! Is that you in there?"

"Yes," Stacey whispered. "But don't tell anyone. Everyone thinks I'm Mark."

"A little joke, huh? Well, you had me fooled. I wondered where you were and why you weren't backstage. Good luck to you, as if you needed it. You're doing a really fine job."

Stacey smiled. Yes, she was doing a good job, she could tell. She was glad to be part of the ballet, even as the Nutcracker.

"Places!" Ida May said again.

Stacey went to the right side of the stage and waited for the curtain to rise. Next to her stood Pam and Lynn, dressed in their snow-flake costumes. Pam was fidgeting with her hair. "Do I look all right?"

"Yes," Lynn said. "Do I?"

"Oh, I hope I don't dance the wrong dance," Pam said nervously.

"Hey, has anyone seen Stacey?" someone asked.

Stacey held her breath inside the mask. Maria looked in her direction. "I'm sure she's around here somewhere. Stacey wouldn't miss the show."

Stacey laughed to herself.

The second scene was about to begin. The Nutcracker had a big part here. While on a magical journey with Clara, he was attacked and wounded by King Rat and many mice.

Onstage, Stacey played the part the best she could. When the mice attacked her, she spun around and fell to the floor. When the lights dimmed, the dancer who played the prince changed places with the Nutcracker, and Stacey disappeared offstage. It looked like the Nutcracker had turned into a prince. The audience applauded.

From offstage, Stacey could watch the rest of the ballet. The prince took Clara through the Kingdom of Sweets, where the Sugar Plum Fairy and other dancers performed. When Maria entered the stage and started to dance, Stacey followed along with her, danc-ing every step in her mind.

After the final act, the curtain came down and the curtain calls began. Stacey lined up with everyone else and took a bow. She was absolutely sure she'd gotten away with the masquerade.

Ida May whispered, "I want you to take another bow. And be sure to take off your head. Everyone wants to see who the magnificent Nutcracker is."

Take off her head? Oh, no, Stacey thought. She felt a wave of panic. She hadn't counted on this. Not only would Pam and Lynn find out who she was, but the entire community would. I'll never live this down, she thought.

When the curtain rose, Stacey stood in the middle of the stage and bowed. Afterwards she tried to run offstage, but Ida May gave her a firm but gentle shove back. "Take off your head!"

Stacey froze in place, unable to do it. Pam and Lynn came running up to her.

"Here, we'll help you, Mark," they said, pulling at the head before Stacey could stop them.

Then the head was off. A gasp came up from the audience. "It's Stacey!" someone said. People cheered and applauded her. She took another bow.

Pam looked startled. "What happened to Mark?"

"Sprained his ankle," Stacey muttered. She couldn't help chuckling to herself. It had been fun fooling people—especially Pam.

After the final curtain call, people from the audience crowded onto the stage. Mrs. Fremple, Stacey's mother, Tommy, and Mark gathered around Stacey, along with a group of small children.

"Please, may I have my picture taken with you?"a little girl asked Stacey.

"Sure," she said and put the head back on.

The girl's father snapped the picture.

"You should wear that mask all the time," Tommy teased. "It makes you look great!"

Stacey's mother hugged her. "I was really proud of you. You carried yourself well, standing straight and tall. You brought real magic to the show."

"I guess it's the spirit that counts," Stacey said. She removed the big head and smiled at Mrs. Fremple.

Mrs. Fremple winked.

"Gee, Stacey, I'm impressed," Pam shrieked, running up to her. "Everyone's treating you as if you were the star!"

"She is," Mark said, leaning on his crutches. "Don't you know, everyone comes to see the Nutcracker!"

Stacey looked at Mark and smiled. Next to him, her mother lifted a camera to her eye.

"Wait!" Stacey told her. Then to Pam and Lynn she said, "Come on. We can all be in the picture together." She put the big Nutcracker head back on and stood straight and tall in the center.

A Note from the Author

For as long as I've known me, I've been tall. From third grade on I was the tallest girl in my class and because of it I slumped. Posture teachers tried to help me stand up straight but ballet classes helped the most, showing me how to carry myself with poise and grace. For ten years I took lessons in ballet, tap, and acrobatics. This education led to a career as a fashion model and a professional dancer on the stage, in motion pictures, and television.

I started writing books after I married and had four sons, but my interest in dancing has continued through the years. At present I'm taking jazz dancing for fun and exercise.

Nancy Robison